2—

D0344362

Sabine Weiss

little angels

Essay by Maira Kalman

Picture This Publications

Los Angeles + New York

© 1997 Picture This Publications

Introduction © 1997 Maira Kalman

All photographs © the photographers
and Estates of photographers

Front cover - © 1997 Jacques Lowe
Back cover - Alexandra Stonehill
Frontispiece - Jack Delano

All rights reserved.
No part of this publication may be reproduced,
stored in a retrieval system or transmitted in any form
or by any means, electronic, mechanical, photocopying, recording,
or otherwise, without prior written permission of
Picture This Publications.

Editors - Marla Hamburg Kennedy and Susan Martin
Design - Marika van Adelsberg
Copy Editor - Sherri Schottlaender

PICTURE THIS
WEST:
520 Washington Boulevard
Suite 280
Marina del Rey, California 90202
310. 315.2889 (tel)
310. 315.2891 (fax)

EAST:
110 Duane Street
New York, New York 10013
212. 240.9007 (tel)
212. 240.0948 (fax)

Distributed by D.A.P.
800. 338.BOOK

ISBN 1-890576-OO-X

Printed and bound by Palace Press
China

Barbara Morgan

When my mother was a green-eyed, gorgeous girl

she would have a tantrum if her burning-hot tea wasn't burning or filled to the brim of her glass. Fling herself on the floor, feet pounding. She demanded (and got) prettier dresses than her sister got. She snuck out in them at night near black and windy trees, to kiss boys. And then she would drop them (the boys) like hot potatoes. And then they

Raymond Depardon

would come slinking around again and more green eyes and more kisses and more hot potatoes.

We called my fat, squinty-eyed cousin, Witch. Just Witch. Witch would pout and cry and turn red and kick and make everybody crazy. She wouldn't share her dolls or her toys and would scream at you at the drop of the hat. And all the cousins knew that she was Trouble. Witch had a favorite bathing suit with daisies all over it. Of course we hid Witch's bathing suit. And she looked for it furiously. And then of course I took my clothes off at the beach and I was wearing it. Well. It was pandemonium.

I did other stinky things. At the crooked age of seven I stole a pearly-pink ribbon from the neighborhood variety store. I got caught. I denied the theft. Insistence by the skinny gray owner. Returning the ribbon, somber slow-motion shame and misery.

At eight, I was a tomboy. Madras shirt, apple, book, stick, knees, socks, sneakers. My older sister was taller, leaner, more serious. We needled each other and ratted and snitched and dug nails in deep. Once I punched her in the chest and at that instant a car backfired and I thought I had exploded her breast.

After marathon Monopoly games, my next-door neighbor Larry Birkner and I would exchange private peeks of private parts. Later, near the tennis courts, after I had kissed Howard Silver's bumpy lips, I hit him over the head with a red umbrella. Surprise.

At Camp Betar where we spent the summer eating blueberry pies and praying on Friday night for I don't know what, I had a fight with the fat, ham-faced Miriam Schneider, who looked exactly like Betty Boop. This was not a verbal argument, but a big flat-out brawl, which ended with her sitting on top of me, pinning me down grunting and grimacing. What the fight was about, of course, is a mystery. I remember our bunkmates standing on the sidelines, cheering on my futile attempts to win. In my mind, I was the heroic one. I was the angel and she was the devil. But of course, she was looking down at me thinking what a weasely devil she had wriggling under her. It's all relative.

I tell you these stories because these things have happened to everyone. To every single child, in every bitsy town on earth. So if you have been in a fight with, let's say, the beastly Fred Crunkle, and have stolen and lied and generally cranked around with your sneaky heart thumping, what constitutes angel? It's not about being starched or polished or cute or polite. Not about how well you behave or how quickly you listen. But in how yearning and alive and vulnerable and ridiculous and mean and tender and irreplaceably epic each child is. It's about having ears that stick out. About breaking yet another glass. About doing stuff and never thinking of the consequences. It's about unruly red hair and braces and fever. It's stealing candy and sharing candy and wearing clothing too big or too small. It's about seeing something for the first time and making a million mistakes and not ever getting completely discouraged.

And you could cry for the beauty and heroism of it all. Now, let's eat some pie, and play hopscotch, and relax.

—Maira Kalman

Genevieve Naylor

Knauer/Johnston

Alexandra Stonehill

Jacques Lowe

Sabine Weiss

Simon Cherpitel

Harry Gruyaert

Nan Goldin

Ernst Haas

Wayne Miller

Bruce Davidson

George Zimbel

Bob Adelman

Roman Vishniac

Knauer/Johnston

Alexandra Stonehill

Jerome Liebling

Larry Towell

Walter Rosenblum

Marc Riboud

Ernst Haas

Jacques Lowe

Jean Gaumy

Wayne Miller

Rebecca Lepkoff

Harry Gruyaert

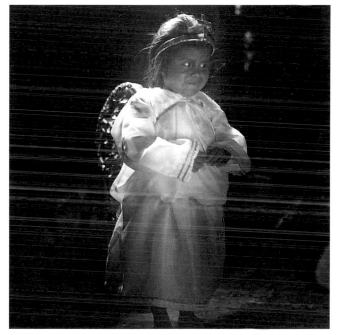

Debbie Fleming Caffery

Jeannette Montgomery Barron

Eve Arnold

Inge Morath

Sabine Weiss

Sabine Weiss

François Robert

Tom Rafalovich

53

Henri Cartier-Bresson

John Vachon

Wayne Miller

Bill Perlmutter

Keith Carter

Bob Willoughby

Arthur Leipzig

Oraien E. Catledge

W. Eugene Smith

Bob Willoughby

Jack Delano

Bruce Davidson

Ernst Haas

Jessie Tarbox Beals

Eric Hamburg

Jean Gaumy

75

Debbie Fleming Caffery

Jacques Lowe

Debbie Fleming Caffery

Elliott Erwitt

Elliott Erwitt

Gertrude Käsebier

Arthur Rothstein

Terry Evans

Arthur Rothstein

Inge Morath

Keith Carter

Lida Moser

André Kertész

Elliott Erwitt

PHOTOGRAPHERS AND CREDITS

Bill Perlmutter